MY BROTHER TOM HAS SUPERPOWER

by
Harriet Axbey

YOUCAXTON
PUBLICATIONS

Harriet Axbey 2021

The Author asserts the moral right to
be identified as the author of this work.

ISBN 978-1-914424-25-0

Illustrations Copyright © Jonathan Raiseborough

Published by YouCaxton Publications 2021
YCBN: 01

YouCaxton Publications
www.youcaxton.co.uk

For My Brother Matthew

My brother Tom has superpowers,
(But don't tell anyone!)
I've watched him now for hours and hours,
And I don't know how it's done.

He looks at someone out at play,
And can tell what's in their head.
He does it almost every day,
I wish it were me instead.

You see Tom has superpowers,
He reads minds- I'm sure it's true!
Don't get too close is my advice,
Or he could read yours too!

He told me when Jack was hungry,
So I then gave him some food.

He told me when Jane was lonely,
So I played tag with her too.

My brother Tom reads people's minds,
He can tell me what they think.
He'll look right at their face and eyes,
And read them in a blink!

Now Tom uses his superpowers,
To help me when I'm confused,

He reads their minds and tells me,
So I know which words to choose.

He's so clever, he can just tell,
How someone's feeling inside.
He doesn't need to scream or yell,
For people to know his mind.

He reads the teachers minds I'm sure,
To do so well in his class,
He uses his power to ensure,
That he always gets a pass!

My brother is so popular,
Everyone is friends with him.

With his mind trick he'll go far,
It is always Tom who wins.

Sometimes it feels like everyone,
Has powers except for me.
They laugh and play and have such fun,
While they all just let me be.

I wish I had powers sometimes.
I'd get all my homework done.
I'd read all of the teachers minds,
And it would be me who won!

I wish I understood the rest,
Of my class that talk all day.
They would laugh and call me the best,
And they'd always want to play.

I wish I had Tom's cool power,
To know what's in someone's mind.
I guess wrong all of the time,
And people aren't always kind.

I told my mum about Tom's skill,
As she tucked me in I said:

"Why does Tom get to be so cool,
That he can see inside of heads?
He's my brother so why don't I ,
Get to read minds instead?"

She stroked my head and said to me,

"You have superpowers too,
It might not be easy to see,
But what matters is what you do.

When Tom said Jane was lonely,
You asked to play with her.
When Tom said Jack was hungry,
You both shared your dinner.

Some see the world differently,
And that's okay now my dear,
But you act so brilliantly,
There's really nothing to fear.

Tom can't read minds and no one can,
That would make the world so dull!

All we can do is guess and learn,
Help each other to the full.

You don't need to see inside their mind,
Your superpower is that you're kind."

Me and Tom have superpowers,
(But don't tell anyone!)
You can watch us for hours and hours,
And we'll tell you how it's done.

ND - #0030 - 071221 - C24 - 210/297/2 - PB - 9781914424250 - Gloss Lamination